Seth Changes His Mind

Written by Tania Nurton
Illustrated by Jo Race

Chapter One

"He shoots...He scores!" Rory waved his arms in the air and ran around the cage singing a victory chant.

"That was a foul! You are such a cheater!" Sam shoved Rory, while the rest of the team crowded round wanting to put their two pennies worth in.

The bell chimed to signal the end of morning break. "Saved by the bell, literally!" thought Seth, as he slipped his sticker book into his rucksack and got to his feet, leaning on his crutches.

"Come on then Seth, let's get you into class before the rush." Mrs Harmer took Seth's rucksack and walked alongside him to make sure he didn't get knocked.

Seth knew that Mrs Harmer meant well and didn't want him to get hurt; but he already felt like an outsider with the other lads in his class. It was bad enough that he had to sit

and sort his football stickers at break while the rest of his friends charged around playing. Having Mrs Harmer two seconds behind wherever he went did nothing to help him fit in.

The next lesson of the day was Maths. The class was tasked with finding things around the classroom to measure. Seth liked the idea of that better than writing sums in his book until lunchtime. They were asked to pick partners and Sam walked over to Seth.

"I wonder how tall the desk is" pondered Seth. "I'll go and get a metre stick." Seth stood up on his crutches and went to grab their equipment.

"Be careful Seth or you'll fall over, I'll get you and Sam a metre stick." Mrs Harmer was only trying to be helpful, but Seth was fed up with people who

kept telling him to be careful. He liked
to do things for himself.

After lunch Seth's physiotherapist,
Rachel, came into school for his monthly physio session. Have you thought
any more about what we discussed last
time Seth?" Rachel had been talking to
Seth about using a wheelchair.

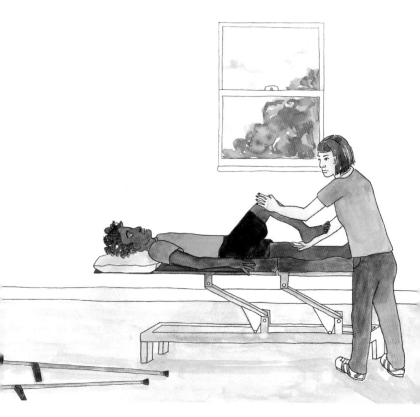

"Just sometimes, Seth, like when you're moving around school or want to go out at weekends. You'd feel safer and wouldn't get so tired." "Um, maybe, I'll think about it. Anyway, I need to get back to class now. It's nearly home time." Seth didn't want to think about it at all, not even for a minute. He didn't see the point. Anyway, wheelchairs weren't for people like him.

The only other person Seth knew who used a wheelchair was his Nan. She used to have a chair when she went out with Seth and his mum. Seth had played in it when he went round to see her, which was fun, but he didn't like the way people treated Nan when she was in the wheelchair.

They used to talk to her as if she was daft. Daft or deaf, Seth wasn't sure, but they spoke really slowly and loudly, as if Nan didn't understand.

One time when Mum left Nan to go and get something in another part of the shop, someone just went up to Nan and pushed her out of the way, as if she was an object; and people used to grab hold of the handles on the back to take her to where they thought she wanted to go, without even asking. The thing Seth really hated was when they asked him or Mum what Nan wanted, as if she didn't have a tongue in her mouth. All in all, Seth really couldn't see why anyone would choose to be in a wheelchair.

Chapter Two

"Can I have two volunteers to take the register down to the office please?" Said Mrs Harmer, slipping the pieces of paper into their plastic wallet. Seth kept his hand down. He didn't see the point, because carry-ing registers was another thing he wasn't designed to do. He needed both hands for his crutches unless he wanted to land in a pile on the floor!

The next day, after early work and before the class started English, Mrs Madeley gathered everyone on the carpet. She said she had something exciting to tell them. Mrs Madeley waited until they were all quiet on the floor and began to speak. "Now children, as you know I'm going to be having a baby in a couple of

months, so I won't be able to teach you for a while as I will need to stay at home and look after the new baby.

The really exciting news is that you're going to be getting a new teacher!" The children started to chatter over each other, buzzing with a thousand questions. Mrs Madeley explained that she didn't know who the new teacher was going to be yet, but that she was sure they would be won-derful and that the chil-dren would have fun with them.

Later in the week, on Thursday night, Seth put his necker on and collected his stuff ready to go to Scouts. Seth was excited to show everyone the lego model he'd built with his Dad when he saw him at the weekend. It had taken them hours but Seth was really pleased with the results.

At Scouts, the children played cor-
ners. Akela suggested that maybe
Seth could help him judge the win-
ners, as he may find the running
around difficult. Then at the end of
the session they all played Chinese
Whispers and the
Shopping List Game.
Seth liked the Shop-
ping List Game as he
thought he had a
really good memory,
but he was still sad
that he couldn't join in
with all the games that
they played at Scouts.

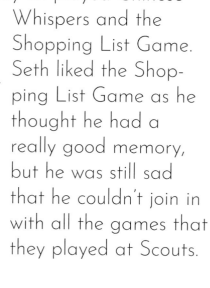

Chapter Three

Two months later, Class 6 were excited to meet their new teacher as they walked into class on Monday morning. The children piled into the classroom noisily speculating about what they would be like. Young or old? Man or woman? Strict or friendly?

They wandered into class and heard a voice. "Carpet places please year 6, lots to do today, let's make it a good one". As everyone filed in it took a moment for them to register what they saw. He was in a wheelchair!

The new teacher fiddled around with the whiteboard and then turned to face the class.

"Good morning year 6, I'm Mr Watkins, and you lucky people have me as your new teacher! Now, first thing's first, you're probably wondering about the cool wheels?

Well I was born with a condition called Spina Bifida, which means I use a wheelchair when I'm not in my own surroundings. If you have any questions please ask and I'll be happy to answer them."

If the children were nervous about what their new teacher would be like then they needn't have worried. Mr Watkins was really funny. He cracked jokes about his wheelchair and never minded if the children asked him how he did things. He said asking questions was always good because it's how we learn.

Seth's mum worked late on Tuesdays, which meant he had to do Stay and Play. That was fine with Seth, as Sam stayed late on Tuesdays too. They compared what football stickers they had and swapped to try and make a complete set. They were both trying to get all of the Manchester United ones.

It was 5 o'clock and Seth was waiting with Mrs Harmer for his Mum to pick him up. "Bye Seth, have a good evening!"

Mr Watkins wheeled up to the door where Mrs Harmer and Seth were standing. He pressed a button on the remote control around his neck and the lights on his wheels lit up. He adjusted the rucksack he was carrying on his lap and zoomed off across the carpark and down the road.

Mr Watkins had explained that he had a special wheelchair for travelling long distances, like to and from school. It had motors in the wheels to do some of the work when he pushed them.

Chapter Four

"Muuum, can we go now?" whined Seth. He had been been watching Bonnie swim up and down the pool for what seemed like forever, and really wanted to get home and watch that Youtube video Sam had been talking about at lunchtime.

"Won't be long now Seth. Here, go and get yourself something from the vending machine".

Seth took the shiny coins from his Mum's hand and wandered down towards the cafe area. As he got closer to the badminton courts he heard a deafening noise and lots of shouting. There was a large group of people in wheelchairs passing a ball around frantically. It looked and

sounded really exciting, so he stopped to watch for a while.

"Right, time out guys, I need water." Seth immediately recognised the person wheeling towards the benches as Mr Watkins.

"Hey Seth, how's it going?" Seth sat there for a second, unsure what to say next. It was always weird seeing teachers out of school. "Ever fancied giving basketball a go Seth? There's a junior league on a Sunday morning!"

"Um, maybe, er I don't know," replied Seth.

Seth's Mum came along and put an arm around his shoulder. "Hello Mrs Kassinanga, good to see you!"

"Mr Watkins, I didn't know you played basketball!"

"Ah well I'm no Ade Adepitan, but it keeps me fit. I've just been telling Seth that there's a junior league on a Sunday morning if he fancies giving it a go."

"What do you think Seth?" said his mum, looking eager.

"Yeah, maybe, but can we go now Mum? I need to finish my Science project." "Genius move!" thought Seth. Mum and Mr Watkins would be really impressed with his new found enthusiasm for Science, and he wouldn't have to let on how uncomfortable and confused he was feeling. Basketball looked kind of fun, but if he started doing that it would be like he was admitting he was different to everyone else. He was one of those, in a wheelchair.

As soon as he got home Seth chucked his bag on the bed and turned on his computer. He opened up his emails and saw the link Sam had been talking about at lunchtime.

Some other boys had seen it and Seth wanted to know what all the fuss was about.

As he pressed play he realised that this new Youtuber was a boy in a really cool red wheelchair with flames on the spoke guards, and he was doing wheelies. He was amazing. Yes, he was different, but not in a bad way. All Seth's friends were obviously really impressed with Whizz Kid, and he had to admit that he agreed.

The next time that Seth's physiotherapist came in for his monthly physio session, he said "I've been thinking, maybe using a wheelchair wouldn't be so bad-just sometimes".

Rachel helped Seth speak to his mum. She said that she was really proud of Seth for making such a grown up decision. A few weeks later they went to the local hospital for Seth to be measured for his wheelchair. Seth was still feeling a little apprehensive, but his mum reassured him that she thought he was doing the right thing. That he'd be able to do more without getting tired, and he'd be able to be more independent. Seth's nerves became excitement.

Chapter Five

The day he had been waiting for had arrived. Seth and his physiotherapist went into the medical room where Seth did his exercises. There waiting in the corner was his new chariot. It was Manchester United red, with red, black and yellow spoke guards and it was all new and shiny. Seth lifted the footplates up and climbed into the chair. He tried to move forward, but veered off to the left. "Don't worry Seth, you're doing great. Just remember, left wheel to go right, right wheel to go left. Both wheels to go forward" and Seth tried again. He was doing it. This was very cool!

"Its tea time!" It was a few days later and Seth was getting used to using the the chair when he felt he needed it. Seth turned off his computer and made his way into the kitchen where Mum was dishing up his favourite, bangers and mash.

His mum handed him the plate. "I was talking to Lola's mum this morning. She's got her arm in plaster, poor thing. Fell off the climbing frame yesterday. Looks like she won't be able to have it taken off until the Summer holidays are over."

Seth was sorry to hear this. Being in plaster was bad enough at any time, but in the Summer holidays was particularly bad timing.

The next day Seth was wheeling through the school gates and saw Lola ahead of him so he caught up to her. "Hey Lola, sorry to hear about your arm."

"Hi Seth. Yeah, it sucks. Probably shouldn't have jumped off the climbing frame".

Lola stumbled as she walked across the playground and Seth noticed something. "Do you want me to tie your shoelace? Don't want you falling and breaking the other arm!"

Lola chuckled. "Yes please. You don't realise how many things you need two arms for until one's put out of action".

Lola put her foot up on Seth's lap and he did her shoelace up before they went into class. It felt good to be able to help someone rather than always being the one being helped.

 # Chapter Six

Seth had had his wheelchair for a few months. Now he was used to it he could hardly remember what life was like before when he only had his crutches or why he'd been so resistant to using one. It was Saturday night, and Seth had been mulling something over. "Mum, can I go and try basketball down at the leisure centre tomorrow morning please?"

Seth's mum was a bit taken aback. She'd asked him before and he'd always dismissed the idea. Nevertheless, she was pleased that he was enthusiastic now.

On Sunday morning Seth went down to the leisure centre with his mum. He sat on the sidelines for a while, feeling a bit shy.

"Hi, I'm Darius," said a curly haired boy, about Seth's age, who approached him. "There's some spare chairs over there if you want to come and join the warm up."

"Seth was a bit unsure, but went over and got into a chair. Darius beckoned him over and he joined his group, who were practicing passes together.

So, what did you think Love, are we coming again next week?" Seth's mum was eager to know how the session had gone.

"Yeah, it was awesome!" Seth talked nonstop all the way home about how much fun he'd had and his new friend Darius.

On Monday Seth and Sam were making their way out to lunch when they heard a voice behind them;

"Sam, Seth, could you give me a hand with these boxes please?" Mrs Harmer was putting away the equipment from the earlier Science lesson. Sam took one box and Seth lifted the other one up and balanced it on his lap.

"How's it going Seth? I hardly see you these days."

"Good thanks Miss", said Seth, smiling broadly. Mrs Harmer had been Seth's teaching assistant since he started in key stage two. Truth be told, he missed her a bit now that he didn't need her help so much, but it had to happen. Seth was starting secondary school soon and wanted to do things for himself without having to ask someone to do it for him. all the time.

Chapter
Seven

One morning before school Seth was in the playground playing tag with his friends. Now he had his wheels he could charge around with all the other children without the adults telling him to be careful.

Mr Watkins beckoned him into the classroom. "Seth, I've been talking to Mrs Griffiths about doing some sessions with the children to try out wheelchair basketball. How would you feel about helping me with that?"

Seth thought for a moment. The old Seth would have said no straight away. He hated doing anything to draw attention to himself and the fact he couldn't do the same things as all the other children. These days he felt differently though. His wheelchair meant he could do most of the

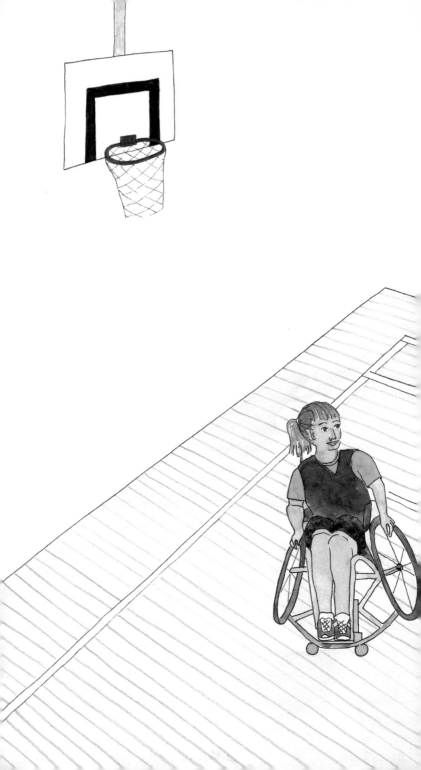

things the other children did, and his friends thought that the chair was cool. So Seth agreed that he'd help Mr Watkins with the basketball sessions.

The big day had arrived. Mr Watkins had arranged for the junior basketball team to lend the school their wheelchairs. As the children walked past the

P.E hall they were buzzing with excitement to do something different that day.

By lunchtime the children were all crowding round Seth. They all wanted to know about Seth's chair, how he used it and why Seth needed to use it to get around. Then some said that they were coming down to the leisure centre on Sunday to try basketball.

Seth forgot about his shyness and didn't know why it had ever bothered him. It was definitely OK to be different!

Printed in Great Britain
by Amazon